THE CHARACTERS IN THE PLAY

THE ENGLISH

King Henry V

Duke of Gloucester
Duke of Bedford — brothers of the King
Duke of Clarence

Duke of Exeter — uncle of the King
Duke of York — cousin of the King
Earl of Westmorland
Archbishop of Canterbury
Bishop of Ely

Richard, Earl of Cambridge
Henry, Lord Scroop — conspiritors who planned to
Sir Thomas Grey — murder the King

Sir Thomas Erpingham
Captain Fluellen
Captain Gower — officers in the King's army
Captain Jamy
Captain Macmorris

John Bates
Alexander Court — soldiers in the King's army
Michael Williams

Bardolph
Nym — camp-followers in the King's army,
Pistol — friends from Henry's younger days
Boy

Hostess, formerly Mistress Quickly — now married to Pistol

THE FRENCH

Charles VI — King of France
Lewis, the Dauphin — heir to the throne
Isabel — Queen of France
Katherine — daughter of the King and Queen of France
Alice — a lady attending on Princess Katherine
Duke of Burgundy
Duke of Orleans
Duke of Britaine
Duke of Bourbon
Charles Delabreth — the Constable of France
Rambures — a French lord
The Governor of Harfleur
Montjoy — a French herald
Ambassadors to the King of England
Monsieur Le Fer — a French soldier

PORTRAIT GALLERY
THE ENGLISH

King Henry V

Duke of Exeter

Dukes of Gloucester, Bedford
and Clarence

Archbishop
of Canterbury
and Bishop of Ely

Richard, Earl of Cambridge, Lord
Scroop and Sir Thomas Grey

Sir Thomas
Erpingham

Michael
Williams

Captain Fluellen

Captain Gower

Captains Jamy
and Macmorris

Bardolph

Nym

Pistol

Hostess
(Mistress Quickly)

Boy

PORTRAIT GALLERY
THE FRENCH

Lewis, the
Dauphin

Katherine

Isabel, Queen of
France

Charles VI,
King of France

Duke of Bourbon

Alice

Duke of Orleans

Montjoy,
the Herald

Rambures

Monsieur Le Fer

Charles Delabreth,
Constable of France

ACT 1

Henry V had just become King of England. Before he was king, Henry had been a playboy, always drinking and partying. Now he was king, he had changed. He was trying to be a good king to all his people.

The Archbishop of Canterbury was worried. The Church had a lot of money, many lands and palaces. Some people thought that the king should take half the money from the Church to help poor people and to run the country.

King Henry thought that he might have a reason to be king of France, as well as king of England. The Archbishop had a plan. The Church could give Henry money to fight a war in France. Henry would be grateful to the Church.

CANTERBURY: The King is full of grace and fair regard.
ELY: And a true lover of the holy Church.
CANTERBURY: The courses of his youth promised it not.

The French ambassador wanted to have a meeting with King Henry.

First, Henry wanted to talk to the Archbishop of Canterbury. Did Henry have a good reason to be king of France? Did he have a claim to the throne?

If Henry had a war with France, many people would get killed or hurt. He had to have a good reason. The Archbishop told Henry that he did have the right to be king of France. He also said that the Church would raise a lot of money to pay for the war.

The Duke of Exeter and the Earl of Westmorland were sure that everyone wanted Henry to fight for the throne of France.

KING HENRY: Now are we well resolved, and by God's help
And yours, the noble sinews of our power,
France being ours, we'll bend it to our awe,
Or break it all to pieces.

King Henry met the messengers from France. He had made up his mind. He had a right to be king of France. He would fight to be king of France.

The messengers brought a present from the dauphin[1].

The present made King Henry very angry. It was a box of tennis balls. It was a joke. The dauphin was really saying that King Henry was still a playboy, not a serious king at all.

King Henry now had another reason to fight for the throne of France. He told the dauphin's messengers that more people would cry about the joke than would laugh about it. He would go to war with France, and wars caused unhappiness.

[1] dauphin – eldest son of the King of France; the next King

KING HENRY: ....many a thousand widows
    Shall this his mock mock out of their dear husbands;
    Mock mothers from their sons, mock castles down;
    And some are yet ungotten and unborn
    That shall have cause to curse the Dauphin's scorn.

ACT 2

King Henry was going to fight the French. His army was gathering at Southampton.

In a poor part of London, Corporal Nym and Lieutenant Bardolph were getting ready to go to France to fight in the war.

They met Pistol and his wife, Mistress Quickly. She was now called the Hostess. Nym had been engaged to Mistress Quickly before she married Pistol. Nym and Pistol were always arguing.

Boy came to tell them that his master, Sir John Falstaff, was very ill. They had all been King Henry's friends before he became king. They used to call him Prince Hal. They had wild parties with lots of drinking. Now Sir John was dying. His heart was broken because the king didn't want to see his old friends any more.

BOY: Mine host, Pistol, you must come to my master – and you, Hostess: he is very sick, and would to bed.

King Henry was in Southampton. Soon he and his army would sail to France.

First, the king had something he must do. He had learned that three of his nobles were planning against him with the king of France. They were traitors[1].

The three traitors were Richard, Earl of Cambridge, Lord Scroop of Masham, and Sir Thomas Grey. Henry gave them each a letter. They thought the letters had good news. Instead, the letters told them they had been found out.

The Duke of Exeter arrested them. They would be put to death for treason[2].

King Henry was very sad. One of the traitors, Lord Scroop, had been his best friend.

The traitors would be punished. It was time to sail for France.

[1] traitors – people who plan against their king, queen or country
[2] treason – the act of trying to harm king, queen or country

KING HENRY: Why, how now, gentlemen?
              What see you in those papers, that you lose
              So much complexion? Look ye, how they change!
              Their cheeks are paper. – Why, what read you there
              That have so cowarded and chased your blood
              Out of appearance?

Back in Eastcheap, Sir John Falstaff's friends were very sad. Sir John was dead.

Sir John's last thoughts were of God. The Hostess, Mistress Quickly, was sure Sir John was in heaven.

It was time for the friends to go to war.

Pistol kissed his wife, Mistress Quickly, goodbye. He told her to take good care of their business, the inn, and to make sure their customers paid their bills.

They all said goodbye and set off for France.

PISTOL: Let housewifery appear. Keep close, I thee
command
HOSTESS: Farewell! Adieu!

The French king was worried. King Henry V of England had arrived in France. The French king was an old man. He remembered past battles with the English: battles that the English had won.

The dauphin wasn't worried. He was quite sure that Henry was still a playboy.

The Constable of France had spoken to the ambassadors who went to Henry's court. The ambassadors told him that Henry had changed. They said he was serious and determined. The dauphin didn't take these warnings seriously.

CONSTABLE: O, peace, Prince Dauphin!
You are too much mistaken in this King.
Question your grace the late ambassadors,
With what great state he heard their embassy,
How well supplied with noble counsellors,
How modest in exception, and withal
How terrible in constant resolution,...

The Duke of Exeter was Henry's uncle, and the most powerful of his nobles. He was Henry's ambassador to the king of France. He brought an ultimatum[1] from Henry.

The Duke told the king that Henry had come to take the throne of France. Through his great-grandfather, Edward III, he had a claim. Exeter showed the king of France Henry's family tree. He called it Henry's pedigree[2]. The French had to agree that Henry was the rightful king of France, or there would be a war.

Exeter also had a message for the dauphin. Henry was very angry about the dauphin's joke with the tennis balls. The dauphin had helped to cause the war.

Finally, the Duke of Exeter warned the French that King Henry had changed. He was not a playboy, he was a serious king.

It was time for the French to make up their minds. The French king would think about it, and give his answer the next day.

[1] ultimatum – final proposal
[2] pedigree – history of family, usually refers to animals

DAUPHIN: .....I desire
                Nothing but odds with England. To that end,
                As matching to his youth and vanity,
                I did present him with the Paris balls.
EXETER: He'll make your Paris Louvre shake for it,...

ACT 3

Henry and his army first landed at Harfleur and attacked the town. They made a siege¹. They dug tunnels under the walls and planted gunpowder. They attacked the town with cannons and made a hole in the great wall of the town.

The siege lasted six weeks. Henry's soldiers were tired. He shouted at them to attack again. He shouted at them to attack bravely. If they charged through the breach² in the wall, they would capture the town.

He made his soldiers want to fight. He made them fight to win.

¹ siege – starving a town or castle by surrounding it and cutting off its supplies
² breach – a hole; a space

KING HENRY: Once more unto the breach, dear friends, once more,
Or close the wall up with our English dead!

Henry's old friends, Nym, Bardolph, Pistol and Boy were at the battle of Harfleur.

They were hanging back. They were afraid.

Captain Fluellen shouted at them to get in the fight.

Afterwards, Boy was thinking aloud. Bardolph was a coward[1]. He and Nym had been stealing. Pistol talked more than he fought. Boy did not want to be with them anymore.

[1] coward – someone who is afraid

FLUELLEN: Up to the breach, you dogs! Avaunt, you cullions.
PISTOL: Be merciful, great Duke, to men of mould!
            Abate thy rage, abate thy manly rage,
            Abate thy rage, great Duke!

Henry's soldiers came from all parts of Britain.

Captain Fluellen was from Wales. Captain Macmorris was from Ireland. Captain Jamy was a Scot. Captain Gower was an Englishman.

They were arguing about different ways of fighting.

Suddenly, they heard the sound of trumpets. The people of Harfleur wanted to talk to King Henry.

GOWER: The town sounds a parley.
FLUELLEN: Captain Macmorris, when there is more better
opportunity to be required, look you, I will be
so bold as to tell you, I know the disciplines of
war;and there is an end.

King Henry told the people of Harfleur that they should surrender[1]. If his soldiers had to keep on fighting, they would do terrible things to the people of Harfleur when the battle was finally over. The king might not be able to control his men.

The dauphin had refused to send help to the people of Harfleur. The Governor surrendered the town to King Henry.

King Henry showed mercy to the people of Harfleur. His soldiers did not do the terrible things he had said.

The Duke of Exeter stayed at Harfleur to make it strong against the French.

[1] surrender – give up

GOVERNOR: The Dauphin, whom of succours we entreated,
Returns us that his powers are not yet ready
To raise so great a siege. Therefore, great King,
We yield our town and lives to thy soft mercy.

Princess Katherine was the daughter of the king of France. She knew that Henry, king of England, had come to France. Perhaps she would meet him. She wanted to learn to speak English.

Her maid, Alice, had been to England. Katherine asked Alice to teach her some English words. Alice pronounced some of the English words in a French way.

Some of the words had rude meanings in French. It wasn't polite for a princess to say such words.

KATHERINE: Excusez-moi, Alice; écoutez - d'hand, de
fingre, de nailès, d'arma, de bilbow.
ALICE: D'elbow, madame.
KATHERINE: O Seigneur Dieu, je m'en oublie! D'elbow.

Henry V

In another part of the palace, the king of France was talking to his son, the dauphin, the Constable of France and the Duke of Britaine.

The king asked all his nobles to join in the fight against Henry. The French were sure they would easily win. They had a big army. Henry's army was small. His soldiers were tired from fighting at Harfleur.

The king sent Montjoy, his herald, to speak to Henry. Perhaps Henry would agree not to fight. If he paid the French a lot of money, they would let him go back to England without a fight.

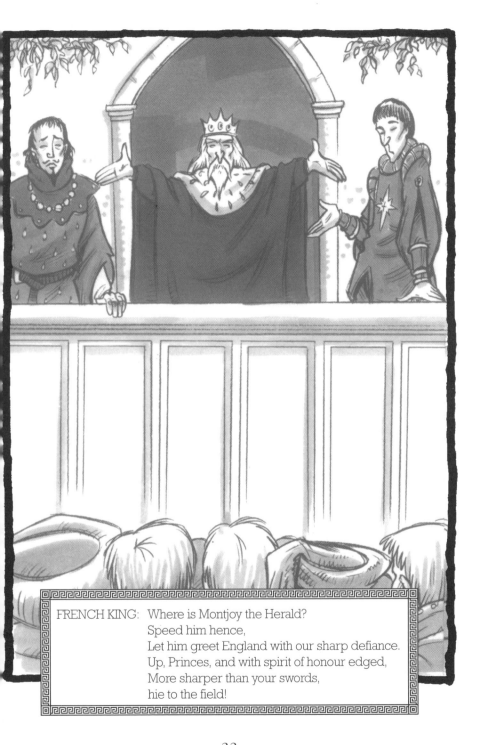

FRENCH KING: Where is Montjoy the Herald?
Speed him hence,
Let him greet England with our sharp defiance.
Up, Princes, and with spirit of honour edged,
More sharper than your swords,
hie to the field!

Pistol met Captain Gower and Captain Fluellen. He was not happy. His friend Bardolph had stolen from a church. The punishment was hanging.

He wanted Captain Fluellen to speak to the Duke of Exeter, to ask that Bardolph not be hanged.

Fluellen thought the hanging was right. There had to be discipline in the army. Soldiers should not steal.

Fluellen told the king about Bardolph stealing from a church. Bardolph had been Henry's friend in the old days with Sir John Falstaff. Now Bardolph was to die.

King Henry agreed with the hanging. He said that anyone who stole from the French should be treated the same as Bardolph.

PISTOL: Fortune is Bardolph's foe, and frowns on him;
For he hath stolen a pax, and hangèd must 'a be –
A damnèd death!

After capturing Harfleur, Henry and his army were marching to Calais. Montjoy, the herald[1] of the French king, brought a message.

The French had not been ready to fight him at Harfleur, but they were stronger now. They had gathered a large army. If Henry paid a ransom[2] and paid for all the damage he had done, he would be allowed to go back to England in peace.

Henry told Montjoy that he would not pay a ransom. He was not looking for another fight. His soldiers were tired. Many of them were ill. Even so, they would not run away. If the French wanted a battle, the English would fight.

Montjoy left to tell the King of France. The Duke of Gloucester hoped there would not be a battle. King Henry said they were not in the hands of the French, they were in the hands of God.

[1] herald – someone who carried messages between important people
[2] ransom – a large sum of money paid because of some kind of threat

KING HENRY: The sum of all our answer is but this:
We would not seek a battle as we are,
Nor, as we are, we say we will not shun it.
So tell your master.

Henry refused to pay the ransom. Without the ransom the French would not let him leave France. There was to be a battle.

The night before the battle, the French nobles were arguing among themselves. The Constable said that he had the best armour in the world. The Duke of Orleans said that he had the best horse.

The dauphin said that his horse was the best. He had even written a poem about his horse.

They wanted day to come so that they could fight. The French nobles felt sorry for the English. They were each going to kill a hundred Englishmen before ten o'clock the next day, or so they thought.....

DAUPHIN: My Lord of Orleans, and my Lord High Constable, you talk of horse and armour?

ORLEANS: You are as well provided of both as any prince in the world.

DAUPHIN: What a long night is this! I will not change my horse with any that treads but on four pasterns.

ACT 4

The night before the battle, Henry had important things to do. He would meet all his nobles to plan for the next day.

First, he wanted to be alone. He needed time to think. He borrowed a cloak from old Sir Thomas Erpingham. Wrapped up in the cloak, he went walking around the camp.

He met his old friend Pistol. Pistol did not know that he was talking to the king. The king pretended to be an ordinary soldier.

Pistol told him how much he loved the king. He was very loyal.

Henry said his name was Harry Le Roy[1]. That was true, in a way. It was good to know that he had such loyal soldiers.

[1] Le Roy or Le Roi is French for 'the king'

PISTOL: The King's a bawcock, and a heart of gold,
A lad of life, an imp of fame;
Of parents good, of fist most valiant.
I kiss his dirty shoe, and from heartstring
I love the lovely bully.

Next, Henry heard Gower and Fluellen talking. They didn't see him. He listened.

Captain Fluellen, a Welshman, spoke good sense. The French were close by, and the English should be careful what they said, and speak quietly. The French were very noisy. That was no reason for the English to behave foolishly. Gower agreed.

Henry realised that he could trust his soldiers to be sensible.

GOWER: Why, the enemy is loud, you hear him all night.
FLUELLEN: If the enemy is an ass, and a fool, and a prating
coxcomb, is it meet, think you, that we should
also, look you, be an ass, and a fool, and a
prating coxcomb?

John Bate, Alexander Court and Michael Williams, three ordinary soldiers, were also talking together that night. King Henry spoke to them.

The soldiers were very worried. Perhaps the king was wrong to be leading them into battle. They had to fight. They could not disobey orders.

King Henry said that each man had to make up his own mind. Something about the way he spoke made them feel braver. Bates said he would fight hard for the king.

Williams and the king had an argument. They exchanged gloves[1]. They would each wear a glove in their helmet to remind them of their quarrel. Williams didn't know that he was wearing the king's glove.

[1] When people exchanged gloves in this way, it meant that they would settle an argument by fighting. The fight was called a duel

HENRY: Give me any gage of thine, and I will wear it in my bonnet: then, if ever thou dar'st acknowledge it, I will make it my quarrel.

WILLIAMS: Here's my glove; give me another of thine.

The soldiers left the king alone.

Henry thought about being king. He had to be different from other men. He sat on a throne. He wore a crown and rich clothes. He often stayed awake at night, worrying about how to keep his country peaceful.

A slave[1] slept better than the king did.

His nobles were waiting for him. First, Henry knelt and prayed. He prayed that God would make his soldiers brave, even though they were outnumbered[2] by the French. He asked God to forgive his sins, and his father's sins.

[1] slave – a person who was sold to another person to do hard work
[2] outnumbered - there were many more French soldiers than English

KING HENRY :O God of battles, steel my soldiers' hearts;
Possess them not with fear; take from them now
The sense of reckoning, if th'opposèd numbers
Pluck their hearts from them.

It was morning. The French nobles wanted the battle to begin. They were sure they would beat the English very quickly.

The Lord Constable said that the English would give up without a fight.

Another noble said that the English horses were tired and weak and thin.

Crows were flying over the English army. Crows like to eat dead bodies. The English would soon all be dead. The crows would have a good meal.

The dauphin was sarcastic[1]. He said they should feed the English army and their horses first. They would put up a better fight.

[1] sarcastic - making fun of something in a cruel way

DAUPHIN: Shall we go send them dinners, and fresh suits,
          And after give their fasting horses provender,
          And after fight with them?

The English nobles were worried. For every English soldier, there were five French soldiers. The French army was fresh, not tired. The Earl of Westmorland wished they had more men.

King Henry spoke to his soldiers. He said that he didn't need any more men. If anyone did not want to fight, he could go back to England. He reminded them that it was the Feast of Crispian[1]. They would all fight bravely that day. It would be a famous battle. They would be proud to tell their friends that they had fought with King Henry on St. Crispin's day. The great battle would be remembered until the ending of the world.

He said that all the soldiers that fought with him that day were his brothers. His soldiers felt very proud. They cheered and shouted for King Henry. They would fight hard for him and for England.

[1] Feast of Crispian – a special day when Christians remember Saint Crispin, a holy man

KING HENRY: We few, we happy few, we band of brothers:
For he today that sheds his blood with me
Shall be my brother;

Montjoy, the French herald, came for King Henry's final answer. Were the English going to fight, or would King Henry surrender to the French king?

King Henry told Montjoy that he was wasting his time. The English would stay and fight. His army had fought hard at Harfleur. They had marched a long way in bad weather. His soldiers were brave. They would not run away.

Henry said the French king could have his body if he was killed. His body would be worthless.

KING HENRY: Herald, save thou thy labour;
Come thou no more for ransom, gentle Herald.
They shall have none, I swear,
but these my joints,
Which if they have as I will leave 'em them
Shall yield them little, tell the Constable.

The battle started. Pistol captured a French soldier. Pistol couldn't speak French but Boy could speak a little. He translated[1] for Pistol.

The French soldier said that he was a gentleman with a nice house. He would pay a ransom of two hundred crowns[2] if Pistol didn't kill him. Two hundred crowns was a lot of money. Pistol agreed. He let the Frenchman go free. The Frenchman was very grateful. He said that Pistol was a knight, and the bravest, most noble lord in England.

Boy was worried. He was helping to guard the camp and the luggage. Only boys like himself were guarding the camp. It was a good thing the French didn't know.

[1] translated – said Pistol's English words in French
[2] crowns – gold coins

BOY: He gives you upon his knees a thousand thanks;
and he esteems himself happy that he hath fallen into
the hands of one – as he thinks – the most brave,
valorous, and thrice-worthy signieur of England.

The French nobles were very unhappy. Everything had gone terribly wrong. They were losing the battle.

There were still enough French soldiers to beat the English, but they were scattered. The French were disorganised.

The Duke of Bourbon went back to the fight. He told the others to follow him. It was better to die than live with the shame of losing to the English.

BOURBON: Shame, and eternal shame, nothing but shame!
Let's die in honour! Once more back again!
And he that will not follow Bourbon now,
Let him go hence,......

The English were winning the battle, but the French were still fighting.

King Henry's cousin, the Duke of York, was dead, and the Earl of Suffolk also. Exeter told Henry how bravely they died.

The French started another attack. The battle wasn't over yet. Henry was worried. He told his soldiers to kill their prisoners.

KING HENRY: But hark! What new alarum is this same? The French have reinforced their scattered men. Then every soldier kill his prisoners! Give the word through.

The French attacked the camp. They killed the boys who were guarding the camp. They burnt or stole the luggage, including everything in King Henry's tent.

King Henry was very angry. He told his soldiers to show no mercy to the French.

Montjoy the herald came for the last time. The French wanted to come to bury their dead. He said the English had won the battle.

There was a castle nearby called Agincourt. The battle would be called the Battle of Agincourt.

MONTJOY: The day is yours.
KING HENRY: Praisèd be God, and not our strength, for it!
               What is this castle called that stands hard by?
MONTJOY: They call it Agincourt.

King Henry met Williams. They had quarrelled the night before the battle and exchanged gloves. Williams was wearing the king's glove in his hat. The king should have been wearing Williams's glove.

He asked Williams why he was wearing a glove in his hat. Williams said that he planned to fight the man who gave it to him. He didn't know that the king had given it to him.

The king decided to have some fun. He told Fluellen to wear Williams's glove. Williams would think Fluellen was the man he quarrelled with the night before.

Sure enough, Williams and Fluellen got into a fight.

The king had to admit it was all his fault. He told Exeter to fill his glove with gold crowns and give it to Williams. Williams was a brave and loyal soldier.

WILLIAMS: My Liege, this was my glove, here is the fellow of it; and he that I gave it to in change promised to wear it in his cap. I promised to strike him if he did. I met this man with my glove in his cap, and I have been as good as my word.

The French and the English were counting the numbers of their dead. A herald reported the numbers to the king.

The French had lost many thousands of soldiers, ten thousand altogether. Among the dead were nobles and princes.

On the English side, the Duke of York, the king's cousin, was dead, and three other nobles. Of all the rest, there were only twenty-five dead.

The king gave thanks to God. There was to be no boasting about the victory by the English soldiers. The victory belonged to God.

KING HENRY: Come, go we in procession to the village:
And be it death proclaimèd through our host
To boast of this, or take that praise from God
Which is His only.

ACT 5

Fluellen was very angry. Pistol had made fun of the leek, the emblem[1] of Wales.

Fluellen told Pistol he had made fun of the leek, now he had to eat a leek. He hit Pistol until he ate it. It was a raw leek. A raw leek was not a nice thing to eat.

Captain Gower told Pistol that he deserved to be punished. Pistol had made fun of Fluellen's Welsh accent. He thought he was not as good as the English soldiers. Now he knew differently. Fluellen had taught him a lesson.

Things were not going well for Pistol. He had learned that his wife, Mistress Quickly, was dead. He decided that he would go back to England and become a thief. There was nothing for him now.

[1] emblem – a symbol

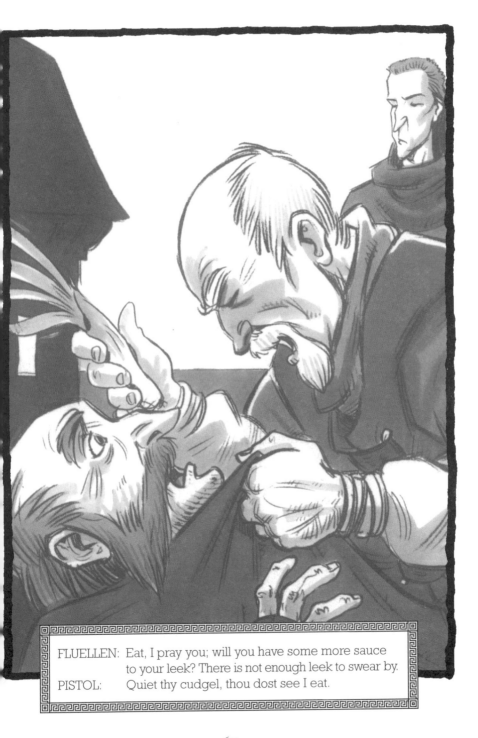

FLUELLEN: Eat, I pray you; will you have some more sauce
          to your leek? There is not enough leek to swear by.
PISTOL: Quiet thy cudgel, thou dost see I eat.

King Henry and his nobles met the French king and queen, their daughter Princess Katherine, and the members of the French court[1].

The French wanted to make peace with Henry. They didn't want any more fighting.

Henry spoke with Princess Katherine. She was very beautiful. He knew a little French. Katherine knew a little English. Her maid, Alice, also translated.

Henry told Katherine that he loved her. He told her that he loved France. He was a plain and simple soldier, not very good at fancy words, especially in French.

He asked Katherine to be his wife. She said that she would do as her father wished. Henry saw that she liked him. They kissed.

[1] the French court – the nobles and officials at the palace of the king

KING HENRY: ...therefore tell me, most fair Katherine, will you have me? Put off your maiden blushes, avouch the thoughts of your heart with the looks of an empress, take me by the hand, and say, "Harry of England, I am thine."

Henry V

The French king agreed to everything the English
wanted. He agreed to the marriage of King Henry and
Princess Katherine. Through their marriage, England
and France would be united.

At this happy moment, it seemed that there would be
peace at last between England and France.

KING HENRY: Now welcome, Kate; and bear me witness all
               That here I kiss her as my sovereign Queen.
QUEEN ISABEL: God, the maker of all marriages,
               Combine your hearts in one,
               your realms in one!